Steadwell Books World Tour
SWEDEN

MARY OLMSTEAD

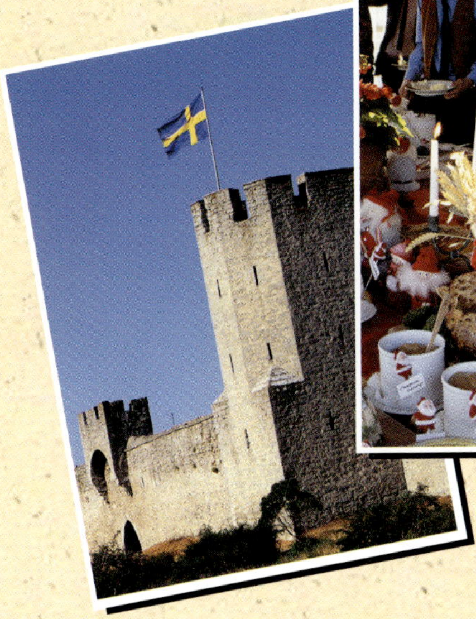

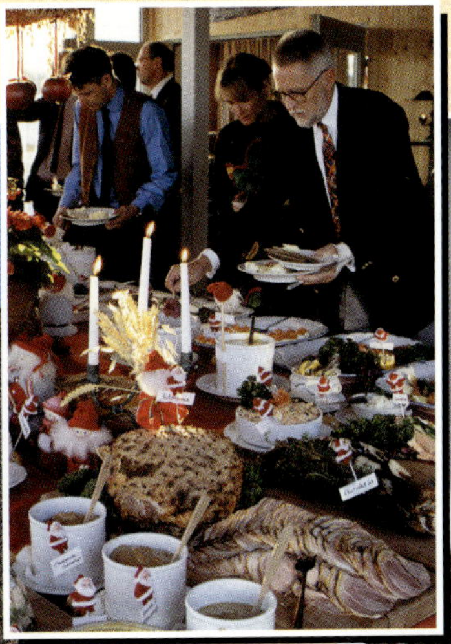

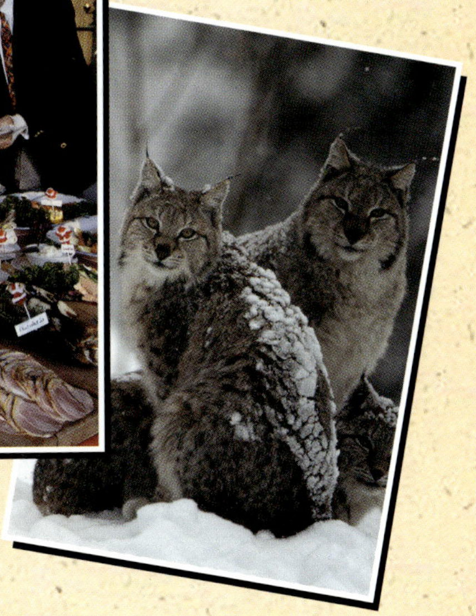

Chicago, Illinois

© Copyright 2004 Raintree

Published by Raintree, a division of Reed Elsevier, Inc.

All rights reserved. No part of this book may be reproduced or utilized in any form or by any means, electronic or mechanical, including photocopying, recording, or by any information storage and retrieval system, without permission in writing from the Publishers. Inquiries should be addressed to:

Copyright Permissions
Raintree
100 N. LaSalle
Suite 1200
Chicago, IL 60602
Customer Service 888-363-4266
Visit our website at www.raintreelibrary.com

Library of Congress Cataloging-in-Publication Data
Olmstead, Mary.
  Sweden / Mary Olmstead.
    p. cm. -- (World tour)
  Summary: Describes the history, geography, economy, government, natural resources, landmarks, and culture of Sweden.
  Includes bibliographical references and index.
  ISBN 0-7398-6817-9 (lib. bdg.)
  1. Sweden--Juvenile literature. [1. Sweden.] I. Title. II. Series.
DL609.O34 2004
948.5--dc21   2003005740
Printed in the United States of America
10 9 8 7 6 5 4 3 2 1 08 07 06 05 04

Photo acknowledgments
Cover photographs by (top, L-R) Stock Image/ImageState, Paul Thompson/ImageState; (bottom) Michael S. Yamashita/Corbis
Title page (L-R) Chris Lisle/Corbis, Bo Zaunders/Corbis, Taxi/Getty Images; content page (L-R) Bo Zaunders/Corbis, Michael Freeman/Corbis; p. 5T Paul Thompson/ImageState; p. 5C The Image Bank/Getty Images; p. 5B Stock Image/ImageState; p. 6 Hulton Archive/Getty Images; pp. 7, 23T Chris Lisle/Corbis; pp. 8, 44T, 44C Bettmann/Corbis; p. 9 Corbis; p. 13T Walter Bibikow/Danita Delimont, Agent; pp. 13B, 42B 43C Felix Oppenheim/Danita Delimont, Agent; p. 14 National Geographic/Getty Images; pp. 15B, 21T, 31B Macduff Everton/Corbis; pp. 15T, 29, 43T Stone/Getty Images; p. 17 Chris Lake/Getty Images; pp. 18, 28 Alex Farnsworth/The Image Works; p. 21B Steve Raymer/Corbis; p. 23B Dennis Marsico/Corbis; p. 24 Francis Dean/The Image Works; p. 25 Pagani Flavio/Corbis SYGMA; p. 27T Philippe Body/BlueBox; pp. 27B, 34 Bo Zaunders/Corbis; p. 31T Ivan Polunin/Bruce Coleman Inc.; pp. 33, 35, 43B Russell Young/Danita Delimont, Agent; p. 37 AFP/Corbis; p. 38T Hubert Stadler/Corbis; p. 38B Michael Freeman/Corbis; p. 38C Taxi/Getty Images; p. 40 Hans Strand/Corbis; p. 41 Dave Bartruff/Corbis; p. 42T Michael S. Yamashita/Corbis; p. 44B Bertil Ericson/AP Wide World Photos

Photo research by Amor Montes de Oca.

Additional photography by Raintree Collection.

CONTENTS

Sweden's Past 6
A Look at Sweden's Geography 10
Stockholm: A Big-City Snapshot 16
4 Top Sights 20
Going to School in Sweden 28
Swedish Sports 29
From Farming to Factories 30
The Swedish Government 32
Religions of Sweden 33
Swedish Food 34
Cookbook 35
Up Close: Norrland 36
Holidays 40
Learning the Language 41
Quick Facts 42
People to Know 44
More to Read 45
Glossary 46
Index 48

Welcome to Sweden

Hej! That's Swedish for hello. Would you like to learn about Sweden? This book is a good place to start, because it will tell you many things about the country and its people. Who knows? After reading about this northern land, you may decide to see Sweden for yourself. In the meantime, prepare to take an imaginary trip to the Land of the Midnight Sun. Ready, set, read!

Reader's Tips:

- *Read the Table of Contents*

In this book, there may be some sections that interest you more than others. Look in the front of the book at the Contents page. Pick the sections that interest you and start with those. Check out the others later.

- *Go to the Index*

Looking for specific information? Look in the Index located in the back of the book. Here you will find a list of subjects that are covered in the book.

- *Use the Glossary*

As you read, you will come across some words in **bold** type. If you do not know their meaning, look them up in the Glossary on page 46. They are in alphabetical order.

◀ **FOLK COSTUMES**
This Swedish girl is dressed in a traditional Swedish folk costume.

▲ **SLEEPING WITH THE LIGHTS ON!**
The northern part of Sweden is known as the Land of the Midnight Sun. From May through July, the sun never entirely sets in this region.

▲ **BACK TO NATURE**
The geography of Sweden is mostly flat in the lowlands, with mountains in the west.

SWEDEN'S PAST

Learning about Sweden's past can make the present come alive. Read on to learn the history of Sweden!

Early Sweden

People did not settle in Sweden until the ice that covered most of the country melted, around 8,000 B.C. The first written record about the Swedes appeared about 100 A.D. It tells us the Swedes were known as the Svear. The word *Sverige* in Swedish means "land of the Svear."

The Vikings

In the 800s, the Vikings established a trading center near present-day Stockholm. These adventurers sailed across the Baltic Sea and up many rivers. They explored the interior of Russia and went as far as Constantinople (now Istanbul, Turkey) and the Caspian Sea.

The Middle Ages

In the late 900s, Christianity brought many changes to Sweden. Church leaders wrote down laws, founded schools, and encouraged the arts. During the 1200s and 1300s, there were constant power struggles between

▶ **FEARLESS VIKINGS!** This is a replica of a typical Viking war longboat. It was used to carry Viking warriors on their raids across Europe.

▲ **VIKING GRAVEYARD**
While these Vikings were buried in the ground, Viking burial ceremonies often involved placing the body in a boat and sending it out to sea.

rulers and nobles. Toward the end of the 1300s, German merchants controlled most of Sweden's trade. They were the richest and most powerful citizens in Stockholm, which became the capital of Sweden in the 1400s.

To oppose the growing power of German merchants, Sweden united with Norway and Denmark. This union was called the Kalmarunion. Each country had separate national councils and recognized each other's existing laws. In 1397, they elected a king to rule the three countries. His name was Karl XIV Johan.

After a period of unrest, Gustav Vasa became king of an independent Sweden in 1523. He weakened the German trade **monopoly** in Sweden, allowing Sweden to become a strong country.

▶ **KING KARL XIV JOHAN**
Even though this Frenchman ruled Sweden, Denmark, and Norway for almost 35 years, he never learned to speak Swedish!

Sweden Expands

By the 1600s, Sweden controlled Finland and Estonia and seized territories from Russia and Poland. Sweden lost most of these territories in 1709, when Czar Peter the Great of Russia defeated Sweden in the Great Northern War.

As Sweden's population increased during the 1800s, farmland became scarcer. Between 1867 and 1886, almost 450,000 people left Sweden. Most of these **emigrants** moved to the United States.

Modern Sweden

During the 1900s, Sweden remained neutral during both world wars. Even though German troops were allowed to cross Swedish territory to reach Norway during World War II, Sweden also provided shelter for many refugees fleeing Germany.

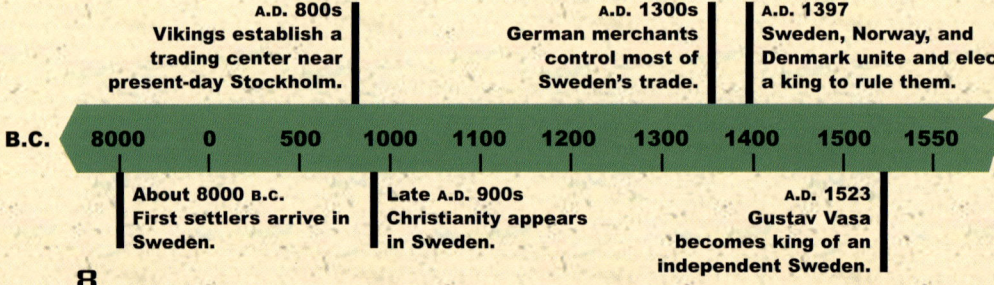

After World War II ended in 1945, Sweden became one of the most prosperous countries in Europe. Through the 1960s, the **economy** continued to grow. A high standard of living spread to all income groups.

In 1975, a new constitution took most of the king's power and gave it to the **parliament** and **cabinet**. Sweden joined the **European Union (EU)** in 1995. The EU is a political and economic organization that promotes cooperation among its member nations.

▶ **ALL ABOARD!** In the 1800s, many Swedes decided to leave their homeland for a new start in America.

A.D. 1945 World War II ends.

A.D. 1995 Sweden joins the European Union (EU).

1600　1650　1700　1750　1800　1850　1900　1950　2000　A.D.

A.D. 1818 King Karl XIV Johan, a French general, becomes king of Sweden.

A.D. 1975 A new constitution takes away most of the king's power.

9

A Look at Sweden's Geography

Sweden is a land of picture postcard scenery. There are glacier-topped mountains, vast forests, and wild rivers. The coastline is peppered with **fjords**, islands, and sandy beaches. In the wilderness areas of the far north, you might travel for hours without seeing a soul. The south has gently rolling hills and lake-studded forests to enchant you. This land of quiet beauty has a magic all its own.

Land

Sweden is situated on the eastern part of the Scandinavian Peninsula. The **peninsula** is located on the northeastern part of the European continent. Norway borders Sweden on the west, Finland lies to the northeast, the Gulf of Bothnia is on the east, and the Baltic Sea is to the south and southeast. To the southwest, the Kattegatt separates Sweden from Denmark and connects the Baltic and North Seas.

Sweden has three main land regions. The largest region is Norrland in the north. It covers about three-fifths of the country. The Kolen Mountains mark Sweden's border with Norway in this land of vast forests. The southern two-fifths of the country include the Swedish lowland and the Swedish highland regions. The lowland is a region of beechwood forests and the rich farmland of the Skåne plains. The third region is Gotaland, which includes the rocky Småland highlands.

▶ **SWEDEN'S SIZE**
Sweden measures 932 miles (1,500 km) from north to south and 250 miles (400 km) from west to east. Western Europe's third largest country, Sweden is almost the same size as California.

Water

Are you a water lover? Then Sweden is the place for you. It has a coastline 4,724 miles (7,602 km) long. Many groups of small islands and two large islands lie just off the coast. The largest islands are Gotland, a fertile island covering 1,160 square miles (3,004 sq km), and Oland, which covers about 520 square miles (1,350 sq km).

Sweden could be called a land of lakes, since it has 90,000 of them! One of the largest lakes in Europe is Lake Vänern. Located in Sweden's southern lowland area, this lake covers 2,156 square miles (5,584 sq km). Other large lakes are Lake Vättern and Lake Mälaren. In the north, mountain valleys are home to many long lakes.

Sweden's longest river is the Torne. Together with its tributary the Muonio, the Torne flows for 354 miles (570 km) on the border with Finland. The Dal and the Klar are other major rivers. The Klar flows into Lake Vänern. Its name changes to the Göta River as it flows out of the lake and empties into the Kattegatt. Most rivers empty into the Gulf of Bothnia. During the Viking **era**, Swedes used these and other waterways to travel to distant lands. They controlled river trade between the Baltic Sea and the Black Sea.

▲ **ROCKY COASTLINES** While much of Sweden's coastline is rocky, many plants and animals call these shores home.

▲ **ROUGHING IT ON THE TORNE** Some adventurous campers have set up camp on the shores of the Torne River, Sweden's longest river.

13

Climate

Sweden's climate is milder in the south compared to the northern part of the country. Winds from the Atlantic Ocean give southern Sweden pleasant but cool summers and fairly mild winters. In July, temperatures average from 59° to 63°F (15° to 17°C), while January temperatures average about 32°F (0°C).

Northern Sweden is much colder, which makes sense when you realize that 15 percent of the country lies north of the **Arctic Circle**. In the far north, summer temperatures generally climb to only 57°F (14°C). In winter it can drop to −45°F (−43°C). Brrrr! Be sure to bring plenty of warm clothes if you venture north of the Arctic Circle.

▲ **FALL EEL PARTIES**
The skies grow so dark in the fall that eels in Swedish rivers can no longer see fishermen's nets, and they are easily caught. Swedes celebrate their large catch of food with an eel-cooking party!

▲ LET IT SNOW!
Because Sweden receives so much snow in the winter, winter sports are very popular. Some interesting ones are snowboarding, dogsled racing, and ice-surfing.

▶ SUMMER
Summer days are long, warm, and light in Sweden.

STOCKHOLM: A BIG-CITY SNAPSHOT

Some people say Stockholm is one of the most beautiful national capitals in the world. Located where Lake Mälaren empties into the Baltic Sea, the city is built on fourteen small islands joined by bridges. An **archipelago** of more than 20,000 islands protects the city islands from the open sea. Its waterways are filled with boats.

Downtown Stockholm

To tour the city's center, you should begin at Stadshuset (City Hall). This is where the city council meets. Once a year, a banquet is held here for winners of the **Nobel Prize**. From the building's tower, you can watch sailboats in the harbor. After you have enjoyed the view, walk over to Kungsträdgården (King's Garden Square). From this little park, you can see the Royal Opera House. Enjoy the fresh air while you watch a life-sized game of chess or listen to free concerts at the center's bandstand.

Old Town

Long ago, Stockholm was just a tiny island village. Today, Gamla Stan, or Old Town, attracts people to its cobblestone streets and little shops. Watch the changing of the guard at noon in front of the royal palace. Then, tour the Riksdag, the Swedish parliament building. There, you will see murals showing different periods of Sweden's history, and you will learn about the Swedish government. Break for lunch at a little café.

Djurgården

Stockholm has an entire island devoted to fun! It is called Djurgården. Hop aboard a ferry in Gamla Stan to get there. At Vasa Museum, see a ship from 1628. It sank in the harbor twenty minutes after it was launched. After 300 years, the ship was raised from the harbor bottom and restored. If you take the tour, you will learn the ship's rules (bread could not be more than eight years old!) and other interesting facts.

▲ CITY OF ISLANDS
Stockholm is known as a city of islands, since it is spread out over 14 little islands.

Don't miss Junibacken, the storybook house. Here, you travel in small carriages through a make-believe world based on popular Swedish children's stories. Next, enter the Nordic Museum to see folk costumes from all over Sweden. Enjoy exhibits on the Sámi, reindeer herders of the north. Be sure to visit the village-life play area on the ground floor.

Finally, head to Skansen. You could spend all day here. This outdoor folk museum has historic buildings collected from all over Sweden—there is a bakery, a glassblower's hut, barns, windmills, and more. People in folk costumes make pottery and do other traditional crafts. Want to see the smallest monkeys in the world? Skansen has a zoo and aquarium. Just watch out for the piranhas! There are many places to picnic, so why not find a quiet spot to eat, relax, and watch people go by? What a great end to a fun day!

Sweden has many places worth seeing, so if you visit, take your time!

▶ WHO NEEDS GLASSES ... when the chess pieces are this big? This game of chess has certainly drawn a crowd in Kungsträdgården.

STOCKHOLM TOP-10 CHECKLIST

Still trying to decide what to see and do in Stockholm? Here is a list of 10 things you are sure to enjoy.

- [ ] See Stadshuset (City Hall) and enjoy a view of the harbor from its tower.
- [ ] Spend time in Kungsträdgården. You might see a life-size chess game while you are there.
- [ ] Head to Gamla Stan, Stockholm's Old Town, to see the changing of the guard in front of the royal palace.
- [ ] Tour the Riksdag, Sweden's parliament building where the government is run.
- [ ] Stroll the streets of Gamla Stan to find a little café for lunch and something sweet for dessert.
- [ ] Head to the island of Djurgården. Go to the Vasa Museum and see the ship that sailed for only 20 minutes before it sank in the harbor.
- [ ] Take a carriage ride through the make-believe world of Junibacken.
- [ ] Enter the Nordic Museum to learn about the Sámi and other Swedish people. Don't leave before you visit the village-life play area.
- [ ] Wander through Skansen, the open-air folk museum, zoo, and aquarium.
- [ ] Before you leave Skansen, find a quiet spot for a picnic and people-watching.

4 TOP SIGHTS

Near Stockholm

After you have toured Stockholm, why not explore some of the many islands of Lake Mälaren and the Archipelago? Many of them have fairy tale-like castles that you can explore. The royal castle of Drottningholm is only half a mile (1 km) west of Stockholm. You can get there by car or by bicycle, but the most interesting way is by boat.

Drottningholm (Queen's Island Castle) is the Swedish royal family's home. It was built during the 1600s. Tour the beautiful lakeside gardens where you can see the world's only theater from the 1700s that is still in its original state. You can see tools once used to make special effects such as wind and thunder.

Would you like to see a Viking settlement? Cruise over to the island of Björkö and see what is left of Birka, an old trading town founded in 760. The village site is surrounded by the largest Viking-age graveyard in **Scandinavia**. A museum includes Viking items that **archaeologists** have dug up and a model village to show life in Viking times.

End the day with a lazy evening sail. Head in the opposite direction to Skärgården (the archipelago). There, thousands of islets, or small islands, dot the clean, clear waters of the Baltic Sea. You will learn why thousands of Swedes take delight in the quiet charm of these waters.

▼ **DROTTNINGHOLM CASTLE, STOCKHOLM**
This impressive structure used to be the home of the Swedish Royal Family. It is over 300 years old!

◄ **BOATING**
Since Stockholm is built on many islands, you can imagine how popular water activities are. Boating is a favorite pastime to many.

Gotland

Gotland, Sweden's largest island, is 78 miles (125 km) long and 32 miles (52 km) wide. Swedes love to spend time on this lovely island in the Baltic Sea. It is easy to see why. This wooded island has a long shoreline with wild cliffs and golden sandy beaches. The water is surprisingly warm for this part of the world, so come on in! You can camp in wooded areas and get around the island on a bicycle. You can see **stalactite** caves or marvel at the strange limestone fossils of ancient sea creatures.

Gotland is one of Sweden's most historic regions. There are hundreds of prehistoric forts, burial mounds, and "picture stones" dating from 400 to 600 A.D. The stones show ships, people, houses, and animals. The island was a trading center before and during the Viking age. There are more than 100 old churches dating from the 1100s to the mid-1300s. You can bicycle around the island and see these sights for yourself, or visit the museum in the walled town of Visby.

Visby is the island's capital. There are cobblestone streets, tiny cottages, and old churches. Because of its mild climate, roses often bloom along the lanes as late as November. If you visit in August, don't miss the costumes and merrymaking during the medieval celebration. You can take part in activities such as coin making, woodworking, and archery.

◀ **VISBY**
The ancient city of Visby was once a Viking stronghold along the Baltic Sea.

FASCINATING FACT
Botanists come from all over the world to study the great variety of flowers that bloom in Gotland. There are 35 different varieties of orchids, a type of flower that thrives in open spaces in the woods.

▶ **ENCHANTED ISLE**
According to an old legend, Gotland was an enchanted island that rose every evening and sank in the sea again every morning.

23

South Sweden and the Kingdom of Glass

It is fun to hike and bike through the province of Skåne, in the southernmost part of Sweden. This is a region of sandy beaches and little towns. Every few miles, you will see beautiful castles. Many of them are surrounded by moats, which are trenches dug around castles and filled with water.

In 2000, a combination bridge and tunnel was completed in Malmö, Sweden's third largest city. Now, you can drive or take the train from Sweden to Denmark and Germany instead of taking the ferry.

The province of Småland is a rocky land of lakes and forests that is not easy to farm. The area became known as the Kingdom of Glass, because many people set up glassblowing factories. This is one of Sweden's most visited areas. A visit to a glassworks will show you how glassblowers use teamwork to blow and shape red-hot glass into beautiful bowls and other objects. Careful! Don't break anything!

▶ **ÖRESUND BRIDGE, MALMÖ**
This historic bridge, opened in 2000, connects Sweden with the rest of Europe.

◄ **HOT STUFF!**
Glassblowing is the art of shaping a mass of glass that has been softened by heat. The glass is shaped by blowing air through it.

▼ **KINGDOM OF GLASS**
In Sweden's Småland province, glass blowing dates back to the 16th century.

25

Dalarna

Dalarna is in the central part of the country. It is considered to be the most typical of Sweden's provinces. A land of forests, mountains, and pure lakes, Dalarna is the favorite place for Swedes to go to celebrate Midsummer Day. Cottages and red farmhouses dot the countryside and hug the shores of its 6,000 lakes. This province has inspired artists, writers, and craftspeople. Two well-loved painters—Anders Zorn (1860–1920) and Carl Larsson (1853–1919)—were inspired by the charms of Dalarna. In the village of Sundborn, you can visit the home of Carl Larsson.

Lake Siljan, the largest lake in the province, is the center of Dalarna's folklore district. Many interesting small towns circle this lake. If you visit Leksand in the summer, you can see a traditional musical put on by the local people and held outdoors. On Midsummer Eve, local people dress in folk costumes and race Viking longboats across the lake.

▲ **LAKE SILJAN**
Measuring 650 miles (1,046 km) long, this is the largest lake in the Dalarna province. It is an ideal region for year-round sports activities.

▲ **DALARNA, SWEDEN**
These festively dressed women are on their way to church in Dalarna. The boat they are in is a replica of Viking longboats and are raced along the lake during Midsummer Day Festivities.

GOING TO SCHOOL IN SWEDEN

Swedish children must attend school from ages six through fifteen. Swedish students study many of the same courses as you do. Elementary school is called the grundskola and is a little different from elementary schools in the United States. In Sweden, these schools go all the way up to the ninth grade.

Everyone in grades four through seven must study English as a second language. Most continue their English studies after that. In the seventh and eighth grades, students begin to choose their own subjects to study. In the ninth grade, they choose one of nine courses of study to follow.

Most students continue their education after completing the grundskola. Some go to three-year secondary schools, which prepare students to go to college, while some students choose **vocational** schools to prepare them for jobs. Sweden has six universities for those who want to attend college.

▲ SPORTING AN EDUCATION
In Swedish schools, sports do not play as large a part of life as they seem to in the United States. Most sports in Sweden are sponsored by outside clubs, not individual schools.

SWEDISH SPORTS

◀ **SAILS AWAY!**
Sailing is very popular in Sweden. Candles scented with creosote, a tar used to preserve the bottom of boats, is a popular Christmas gift among Swedes!

As you might imagine, winter sports are very popular in Sweden, especially skiing and hockey. There are plenty of places for downhill skiing and snowboarding, and miles of forested trails for cross-country skiing. Thousands of Swedes compete in a 55-mile (89 km) cross-country ski race called the Vasa Race every March. They also like långfärdsskridskoåkning, or long-distance skating. Skaters strap skate blades onto their boots and skate for miles. Swedes also like to play soccer and tennis. There are many tennis courts, both indoor and outdoor, and regular tennis competitions, such as the Stockholm Open. There is even a tennis tournament for children ages eleven to fifteen called the Donald Duck Cup. Sweden is a country of great natural beauty, and its people are very fond of the great outdoors. Swedes go out to the country for camping, hiking, canoeing, and other activities, such as hunting and ice fishing.

FROM FARMING TO FACTORIES

In Sweden, people work at many different types of jobs that people all over the world do—there are shopkeepers, bankers, teachers, day-care workers, and taxi drivers, to name a few.

Swedish industries manufacture many products that are exported around the world. They produce high-quality steel, which is used to make automobiles, jet engines, and many kinds of tools.

Sweden has many large corporations that make electrical and electronic equipment and machine parts. Other products manufactured in Sweden are office machinery, furniture, telephone equipment, and glass products. Forestry products, such as timber, paper, and furniture, make up almost one-fifth of exported goods.

Less than 4 percent of Swedes work in agriculture. Rich farmland is located in the south and central regions of the country. Most farms are small to medium in size and are family owned. Farmers grow many kinds of food, but the major crops are barley, oats, wheat, sugar beets, potatoes, and hay. In the north, Lapps, also called the Sámi, look after large herds of reindeer. Throughout the country, the skills of artisans—woodcarvers, weavers, leather workers, and glassblowers—are valued highly.

▲ **REINDEER HERDING**
About 10% of the Sámi in Sweden make a living by reindeer herding. According to Swedish law, herding can only be carried on by Sámi.

▲ **VOLVO FACTORY**
This woman is working hard at the Volvo factory, a popular Swedish car maker. With locations all over the world, Volvo employs more than 79,000 people.

31

THE SWEDISH GOVERNMENT

Sweden is a constitutional monarchy, which means that a king or queen shares power with elected leaders. There is a **prime minister**, a cabinet, and a **parliament.** A change to Sweden's constitution in 1974 took away most of the monarch's power and gave it to the Riksdag (parliament) and the cabinet, which is a body of advisors to the prime minister. The Riksdag has 349 members who are elected to serve four-year terms. The prime minister is the chief leader and the one who works with the cabinet of ministers to make decisions about how to govern the country. During the 1900s, a welfare-state system was developed that provides many benefits to its citizens. It gives financial help to the unemployed, the ill, and the elderly.

SWEDEN'S NATIONAL FLAG

A yellow cross sits off-center in a field of blue. This design is based on the Scandinavian cross, which is taken from the flag of Denmark. The blue and yellow colors may have been inspired by the national coat of arms, which was developed in the 1300s.

RELIGIONS OF SWEDEN

◀ **LUTHERANISM** Lutheranism is the most practiced religion in Sweden. This type of Christianity was founded in the 16th century.

In Sweden, most people are Christians. They follow the teachings of Jesus found in the New Testament of the Bible. About 94 percent of the population are Lutherans who belong to the Church of Sweden. Lutheranism is a form of Christianity and was the country's official religion from the 1500s to the late 1900s. By 2000, the Church of Sweden was no longer Sweden's official church. This change was made because the Swedish people realized that their population now included people from other countries who have a variety of different faiths and beliefs.

33

SWEDISH FOOD

Sweden is most famous for the smörgåsbord, an assortment of hot and cold foods placed on a large table and served buffet style. Buffet style means each person goes to the table and fills his or her own plate.

A standard meal, however, is usually something simple, such as sausage and potatoes or pyttipanna, which means "bits in the pan." This dish is a beef and potato hash topped with a fried egg. Soups and sauces are often seasoned with fresh dill, a spice that is also used in preserving food. Meat, fish, and vegetables preserved with pickling spices and salt are common in traditional Swedish cooking. This method of preserving food goes back to the days when these types of foods were all people had to eat during the long, cold winters. Fish is another Swedish specialty. It is served fresh, smoked, or pickled. Swedish desserts and baked goods are known around the world for their wonderful taste and variety.

▶ **DIG IN!**
The smörgåsbord comes from two Swedish words: smörgås, meaning "open sandwich," and bord, meaning "table."

COOKBOOK

Swedish Recipe

OLD-FASHIONED FRUIT SOUP DESSERT (FRUKTSOPPA)

Ingredients:
3/4 cup dried apricots
3/4 cup dried prunes
6 cups cold water
1 cinnamon stick
2 slices of lemon, 1/4 inch thick
3 tbs quick-cooking tapioca
1 cup sugar
2 tbs raisins
1 tbs dried currants
1 tart cooking apple, peeled, and cut into 1/2 inch slices

Directions:
- Soak the dried apricots and prunes in 6 cups of cold water for 30 minutes in a 3-quart saucepan.
- Add the cinnamon stick, lemon slices, tapioca, and sugar. Bring to a boil. Reduce the heat, cover, and simmer for 10 minutes, stirring occasionally.
- Stir in the raisins, currants, and apple slices and simmer another 5 minutes, or until apples are tender.
- Pour the contents into a large serving bowl and let cool.
- Remove the cinnamon stick, cover with plastic wrap, and chill in refrigerator.
- Serve the fruit soup in dishes or small bowls.

WARNING
Never cook or bake by yourself. Be sure to have an adult assist you in the kitchen.

UP CLOSE: NORRLAND

Norrland is the name for the northern half of Sweden. It makes up more than half the country, stretching for 625 miles (1,000 km) from north to south. To the west, there are mountain ranges, and to the east is a coastline that is wild and rocky. In between are miles of forest and marshlands.

A Place of Beauty

Sweden's highest mountain, Kebnekaise, rises 7,000 feet (2,133 m), but if you want to climb it, be aware that the weather can change rapidly. If a storm moves in, temperatures can drop to zero quickly, even on a sunny June day!

Above the Arctic Circle, the sun shines from the end of May to mid-July. It never gets completely dark, which is why it is called the Land of the Midnight Sun. In the winter it is the opposite—there are weeks on end when the sun never appears! People come to Norrland to view the northern lights. Green streamers and arcs of light dance in the night sky. This heavenly lightshow is also called the aurora borealis.

Farther back in time, the Sámi (Lapps) followed plentiful herds of reindeer. Today, much of this land is protected as nature reserves or national parks.

Sarek National Park is Sweden's most-loved national park. It represents the best of the far north country. There are mountain peaks, glaciers, green meadows, a river,

▲ AURORA BOREALIS
Like a neon sign, auroral light is produced by an electrical discharge. The light is the glow from atoms and molecules in the earth's upper atmosphere.

▲ **SAREK NATIONAL PARK**
This is the most visited park in Lappland. Mt. Njulla is found here. You can take a cable car to the top for a perfect view over Lake Torneträsk.

◀ **THE ICE HOTEL**
The world's largest igloo is open for business from December through April. It melts away and is rebuilt every year. It is made of snow, ice, and sheet metal. Guest beds are sleeping bags piled on top of reindeer skins and spruce boughs.

swamps, and forests. Elk, bears, wolverines, lynx, hare, Arctic foxes, and many birds inhabit this beautiful land. Visitors to the park must hike in, since there are no roads and no tourist facilities. The weather is unpredictable and the conditions are dangerous in the winter and spring, because of avalanches and snowstorms.

The Sámi

    The Sámi have lived as **nomads** in northern Scandinavia and northwestern Russia for hundreds of years. Many Sámi followed plentiful herds of reindeer and others made a living fishing. In 1986, a nuclear accident in Russia polluted their land and the food that fed the reindeer. It forced the Sámi to find other ways to make a living.

    Today, the Sámi try to follow their old ways. Some still herd reindeer for a living, but they might use helicopters to do it. The shrinking open spaces are forcing the younger generation to make their living in other ways. Some move to the cities, while others stay to work in forestry or to make traditional arts and crafts to sell to tourists. Most Sámi live in houses now instead of traditional **wigwams.** Local schools teach children the Sámi language and culture.

HOLIDAYS

Three holidays make December a festive month. St. Lucia Day on December 13 celebrates the coming of Christmas. A young girl representing Lucia wears a crown of lighted candles. She leads a procession of singing children dressed in white robes. On Christmas Eve, families gather for dinner and exchange presents afterwards. On New Year's Eve, people get together to have fun, just like you, your family, and your friends might. They often set off fireworks.

A **pagan** holiday called the Feast of Valborg, or Walpurgis Night, is celebrated on April 30. This holiday is especially popular with university students who celebrate the end of winter with bonfires and fireworks. June 6 is Flag Day, Sweden's national holiday. On this day, the king presents the national flag in a special ceremony.

Sweden's biggest holiday—Midsummer—is usually celebrated on the first Friday after June 21, around the time of the summer **solstice**. Folk dancers decorate and then raise a maypole, which is a pole that represents the unity of an ancient god and goddess. There is music, dancing, eating, and drinking. Many people stay up all night just to sing and dance around the maypole!

▶ **MIDSUMMER CELEBRATION!** These Swedes are celebrating the first day of summer and warmer weather!

LEARNING THE LANGUAGE

English	Swedish	How to say it
Yes	Ja	yah
No	Nej	nay
Please	Vahr vänlig	VAR-von-leeg
Hello	Hej *or* God dag	Hayj Good-DAHG
Goodbye	Hej då	Ah-YOO
Thank you very much	Tack så mycket	Tahk-soh-MEE-keh
You're welcome	Var så god	Vahr-shoh-GOO
Swedish	Svenska	SVEN-ska

QUICK FACTS

SWEDEN

Capital ▶
Stockholm

Borders
Norway (W)
Finland (NE)
Gulf of Bothnia (E)
Baltic Sea (SE)
The Kattegat (SE)
(strait that connects the Baltic and North Seas)

Area
173,732 sq miles
(449,964 sq km)

Population
8,876,744

Largest Cities
Stockholm (1,626,000)
Göteborg (778,000)
Malmö (250,000)
Uppsala (170,000)

Religions Practiced in Sweden
Christianity, Judaism, Islam

◀ **Sweden's Highest Mountain**
Mount Kebnekaise
(6,946 feet/2,117 m)

▲ **Flag of Sweden**

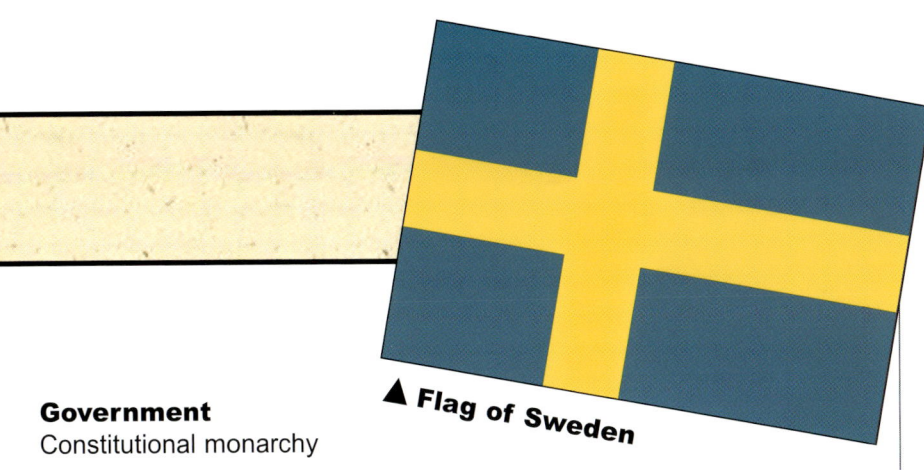

Government
Constitutional monarchy

Literacy Rate
100%

Major Industries
Mining, timber, tourism, steel manufacturing

Chief Crops
Grains, sugar beets, potatoes

Natural Resources
Iron ore, lumber, copper, lead, zinc, uranium

▼ **Coastline**
4,724 miles (7,602 km)

◀ **Longest River**
Torne River 354 miles (570 km)

◀ **Monetary Unit**
Krona

43

PEOPLE TO KNOW

◀ CARL LINNAEUS (1707–1778)

Carl von Linné (born Linnaeus) worked on scientifically classifying plants, animals, and minerals. During the 1700s he traveled around Sweden, gathering his observations on the natural world. He developed a system to organize living things. The natural sciences still use his system today.

▶ ALFRED NOBEL (1833–1896)

Alfred Nobel was a chemist who invented dynamite in the 1800s. After his death, he surprised the world by announcing in his will the creation of the Nobel Prizes. These highly respected prizes are awarded each year to those who have benefited humankind in the year before.

▼ ASTRID LINDGREN (1907–2002)

Astrid Lindgren is Sweden's best-known children's writer. Born in 1907, she is the author of the *Pippi Longstocking* books about a girl who is very strong, lives independent of adults, and does just what she likes. Her books have been translated into more than 50 languages. One of Sweden's most popular tourist attractions is Astrid Lindgren's Värld, a theme park based on the *Pippi Longstocking* books.

MORE TO READ

Want to know more about Sweden? One of these books might be of interest to you.

Anderson, Margaret J. *Carl Linnaeus: Father of Classification. Great Minds of Science* series. Berkeley Heights, N.J.: Enslow Publishers, 1997.

Learn more about this famous Swedish scientist.

Carlson, Bo Kage. *Sweden. Country Fact Files* series. Chicago: Raintree, 1999.

Another great title to provide you with a deeper understanding of the culture and history of Sweden.

Dobson, Mary. *Vile Vikings. Smelly Old History* series. Oxford, U.K.: Oxford University Press, 1998.

Take to the seas with this scratch-and-sniff book and get a whiff of life aboard the Vikings' famous longships.

Fiction

Lagerlof, Selma. *The Wonderful Adventures of Nils.* Iowa City, Iowa: Penfield Press, 2000.

This fun book tells the adventures of a mischievous 14-year-old who is changed into a tiny being, is transported across the Swedish countryside on the back of a goose, and learns about nature, geography, and folklore.

GLOSSARY

Arctic Circle—an imaginary line circling the globe that marks the far northern part of the Earth

Archaeologist—scientist who digs in ancient areas to learn about the way people lived long ago

Archipelago—a group of islands

Botanist—a scientist that studies plants

Cabinet—a group of government officials that advise a president or prime minister

Economy—system of goods and services in a country, especially relating to money

Emigrants—people who leave their country and settle somewhere else

Era—a period of time in history

European Union (EU)—organization of several European countries that have common political and economic aims and interests

Fjord—narrow passage of the sea between cliffs

Monopoly—when one person or group controls a whole section of an economy

Nobel Prize—a prize awarded to people who have benefited mankind in the previous year

Nomads—people who move from place to place

Pagan—a follower of an ancient religion that believed in more than one god

Parliament—an elected group of people who make up the laws in their country

Peninsula—portion of land nearly surrounded by water

Prime minister—head of state, similar to a president

Scandinavia—area that is made up of Sweden, Denmark, Norway, Finland, and Iceland

Solstice—either of the two days in the year when the earth is at its farthest distance from the sun

Stalactite—calcium deposit that looks like an icicle hanging from the top or sides of a cave

Vocational—a school that trains someone in a skill or trade

Wigwams—huts made of sticks, mud, or branches

INDEX

Arctic Circle 14, 36
aurora borealis (See
  northern lights)

Baltic Sea 6, 10, 12, 16, 20, 22

Christianity 6, 33

Dalarna province 26
Djurgården 17

European Union (EU) 9

Feast of Valborg (See
  Walpurgis Night)

glassworks 24, 30
Gotaland 10
Gotland island 12, 22
Great Northern War 8

Kalmarunion 7
Kebnekaise mountain 36

Lake Siljan 26
Lake Vänern 12
Lapps (See Sámi)

Midsummer 26, 40

Nobel Prize 16
Norrland 10, 36
northern lights 36

Oland island 12

Sámi 18, 30, 36, 39
Sarek National Park 36, 39
Scandinavian Peninsula 10
Skåne province 10, 24
Småland province 10, 24
St. Lucia Day 40
Stockholm 6, 7, 16-17
Svear 6

Torne River 12

Vikings 6, 12, 20, 22

Walpurgis Night 40
wildlife 36, 39
World War II 9